METAMORPHOSIS

METAMORPHOSIS

Franz Kafka

Translated by
David Wyllie

GYAN

ISBN : 978-81-212-9024-1 (HB)

First Published, 1915

Indian Reprint in 2017

Published by

GYAN

Gyan Publishing House
5, Ansari Road
Daryaganj, New Delhi-110002
Phone: 9811692060
E-mail: books@gyanbooks.com

Printed at: G. Print Process, Delhi.

I

One morning, when Gregor Samsa woke from troubled dreams, he found himself transformed in his bed into a horrible vermin. He lay on his armour-like back, and if he lifted his head a little he could see his brown belly, slightly domed and divided by arches into stiff sections. The bedding was hardly able to cover it and seemed ready to slide off any moment. His many legs, pitifully thin compared with the size of the rest of him, waved about helplessly as he looked.

"What's happened to me?" he thought. It wasn't a dream. His room, a proper human room although a little too small, lay peacefully between its four familiar walls. A collection of textile samples lay spread out on the table - Samsa was a travelling salesman - and above it there hung a picture that he had recently cut out of an illustrated magazine and housed in a nice, gilded frame. It showed a lady fitted out with a fur hat and fur boa who sat upright, raising a heavy fur muff that covered the whole of her lower arm towards the viewer.

Gregor then turned to look out the window at the dull weather. Drops of rain could be heard hitting the pane, which made him feel quite sad. "How about if I sleep a little bit longer and forget all this nonsense", he thought, but that was something he was unable to do because he was used to sleeping on his right, and in his present state couldn't get into that position. However hard he threw himself onto his right, he always rolled back to where he was. He must have tried it a hundred times, shut his eyes so that he wouldn't have to look at the floundering legs, and only stopped when he began to feel a mild, dull pain there that he had never felt before.

"Oh, God", he thought, "what a strenuous career it is that I've chosen! Travelling day in and day out. Doing business like this takes much more effort than doing your own business at home, and on top of that there's the curse of travelling, worries about making train connections, bad and irregular food, contact with different people all the time so that you can never get to know anyone or become friendly with them. It can all go to Hell!" He felt a slight itch up on his belly; pushed himself slowly up on his back towards the headboard so that he could lift his head better; found where the itch was, and saw that it was covered with lots of little white spots which he didn't know what to make of; and when he tried to feel the place with one of his legs he drew it quickly back because as soon as he touched it he was overcome by a cold shudder.

He slid back into his former position. "Getting up early all the time", he thought, "it makes you stupid. You've got to get enough sleep. Other travelling salesmen live a life of luxury. For instance, whenever I go back to the guest house during the morning to copy out the contract, these gentlemen are always still sitting there eating their breakfasts. I ought to just try that with my boss; I'd get kicked out on the spot. But who knows, maybe that would be the best thing for me. If I didn't have my parents to think about I'd have given in my notice a long time ago, I'd have gone up to the boss and told him just what I think, tell him everything I would, let him know just what I feel. He'd fall right off his desk! And it's a funny sort of business to be sitting up there at your desk, talking down at your subordinates from up there, especially when you have to go right up close because the boss is hard of hearing. Well, there's still some hope; once I've got the money together to pay off my parents' debt to him - another five or six years I suppose - that's definitely what I'll do. That's when I'll make the big change. First of all though, I've got to get up, my train leaves at five."

And he looked over at the alarm clock, ticking on the chest of drawers. "God in Heaven!" he thought. It was half past six and the hands were quietly moving forwards, it was even later than half past, more like quarter to seven. Had the alarm clock not rung? He could see from the bed that it had been set for four o'clock as it should have been; it certainly must have rung. Yes, but was it possible to quietly sleep through that furniture-rattling noise? True, he had not slept peacefully, but probably all the more deeply because of that. What should he do now? The next train went at seven; if he were to catch that he would have to rush like mad and the collection of samples was still not packed, and he did not at all feel particularly fresh and lively. And even if he did catch the train he would not avoid his boss's anger as the office assistant would have been there to see the five o'clock train go, he would have put in his report about Gregor's not being there a long time ago. The office assistant was the boss's man, spineless, and with no understanding. What about if he reported sick? But that would be extremely strained and suspicious as in fifteen years of service Gregor had never once yet been ill. His boss would certainly come round with the doctor from the medical insurance company, accuse his parents of having a lazy son, and accept the doctor's recommendation not to make any claim as the doctor believed that no-one was ever ill but that many were workshy. And what's more, would he have been entirely wrong in this case? Gregor did in fact, apart from excessive sleepiness after sleeping for so long, feel completely well and even felt much hungrier than usual.

He was still hurriedly thinking all this through, unable to decide to get out of the bed, when the clock struck quarter to seven. There was a cautious knock at the door near his head. "Gregor", somebody called - it was his mother - "it's quarter to seven. Didn't you want to go somewhere?" That gentle voice! Gregor was shocked when he heard his own voice answering, it could hardly be recognised as the voice he had had before. As if from deep inside him, there was a painful and uncontrollable squeaking mixed in with it, the words could be made out at first but then there was a sort of echo which made them unclear, leaving the hearer unsure whether he had heard properly or not. Gregor had wanted to give a full answer and explain everything, but in the circumstances contented himself with saying: "Yes, mother, yes, thank-you, I'm getting up now." The change in Gregor's voice probably could not be noticed outside through the wooden door, as his mother was satisfied with this explanation and shuffled away. But this short conversation made the other members of the family aware that Gregor, against their expectations was still at home, and soon his father came knocking at one of the side doors, gently, but with his fist. "Gregor, Gregor", he called, "what's wrong?" And after a short while he called again with a warning deepness in his voice: "Gregor! Gregor!" At the other side door his sister came plaintively: "Gregor? Aren't you well? Do you need anything?" Gregor answered to both sides: "I'm ready, now", making an effort to remove all the strangeness from his voice by enunciating very carefully and putting long pauses between each, individual word. His father went back to his breakfast, but his sister whispered: "Gregor, open the door, I beg of you." Gregor, however, had no thought of opening the door, and instead congratulated himself for his cautious habit, acquired from his travelling, of locking all doors at night even when he was at home.

The first thing he wanted to do was to get up in peace without being disturbed, to get dressed, and most of all to have his breakfast. Only then would he consider what to do next, as he was well aware that he would not bring his thoughts to any sensible conclusions by lying in bed. He remembered that he had often felt a slight pain in bed, perhaps caused by lying awkwardly, but that had always turned out to be pure imagination and he wondered how his imaginings would slowly resolve themselves today. He did not have the slightest doubt that the change in his voice was nothing more than the first sign of a serious cold, which was an occupational hazard for travelling salesmen.

It was a simple matter to throw off the covers; he only had to blow himself up a little and they fell off by themselves. But it became difficult after that, especially as he was so exceptionally broad. He would have used his arms and his hands to push himself up; but instead of them he only had all those little legs continuously moving in different directions, and which he was moreover unable to control. If he wanted to bend one of them, then that was the first one that would stretch itself out; and if he finally managed to do what he wanted with that leg, all the others seemed to be set free and would move about painfully. "This is something that can't be done in bed", Gregor said to himself, "so don't keep trying to do it".

The first thing he wanted to do was get the lower part of his body out of the bed, but he had never seen this lower part, and could not imagine what it looked like; it turned out to be too hard to move; it went so slowly; and finally, almost in a frenzy, when he carelessly shoved himself forwards with all the force he could gather, he chose the wrong direction, hit hard against the lower bedpost, and learned from the burning pain he felt that the lower part of his body might well, at present, be the most sensitive.

So then he tried to get the top part of his body out of the bed first, carefully turning his head to the side. This he managed quite easily, and despite its breadth and its weight, the bulk of his body eventually followed slowly in the direction of the head. But when he had at last got his head out of the bed and into the fresh air it occurred to him that if he let himself fall it would be a miracle if his head were not injured, so he became afraid to carry on pushing himself forward the same way. And he could not knock himself out now at any price; better to stay in bed than lose consciousness.

It took just as much effort to get back to where he had been earlier, but when he lay there sighing, and was once more watching his legs as they struggled against each other even harder than before, if that was possible, he could think of no way of bringing peace and order to this chaos. He told himself once more that it was not possible for him to stay in bed and that the most sensible thing to do would be to get free of it in whatever way he could at whatever sacrifice. At the same time, though, he did not forget to remind himself that calm consideration was much better than rushing to desperate conclusions. At times like this he would direct his eyes to the window and look out as clearly as he could, but unfortunately, even the other side of the narrow street was enveloped in morning fog and the view had little confidence or cheer to offer him. "Seven o'clock, already", he said to himself when the clock struck again, "seven o'clock, and there's still a fog like this." And he lay there quietly a while longer, breathing lightly as if he perhaps expected the total stillness to bring things back to their real and natural state.

But then he said to himself: "Before it strikes quarter past seven I'll definitely have to have got properly out of bed. And by then somebody will have come round from work to ask what's happened to me as well, as they open up at work before seven o'clock." And so he set himself to the task of swinging the entire length of his body out of the bed all at the same time. If he succeeded in falling out of bed in this way and kept his head raised as he did so he could probably avoid injuring it. His back seemed to be quite hard, and probably nothing would happen to it falling onto the carpet. His main concern was for the loud noise he was bound to make, and which even through all the doors would probably raise concern if not alarm. But it was something that had to be risked.

When Gregor was already sticking half way out of the bed - the new method was more of a game than an effort, all he had to do was rock back and forth - it occurred to him how simple everything would be if somebody came to help him. Two strong people - he had his father and the maid in mind - would have been more than enough; they would only have to push their arms under the dome of his back, peel him away from the bed, bend down with the load and then be patient and careful as he swang over onto the floor, where, hopefully, the little legs would find a use. Should he really call for help though, even apart from the fact that all the doors were locked? Despite all the difficulty he was in, he could not suppress a smile at this thought.

After a while he had already moved so far across that it would have been hard for him to keep his balance if he rocked too hard. The time was now ten past seven and he would have to make a final decision very soon. Then there was a ring at the door of the flat. "That'll be someone from work", he said to himself, and froze very still, although his little legs only became all the more lively as they danced around. For a moment everything remained quiet. "They're not opening the door", Gregor said to himself, caught in some nonsensical hope. But then of course, the maid's firm steps went to the door as ever and opened it. Gregor only needed to hear the visitor's first words of greeting and he knew who it was - the chief clerk himself. Why did Gregor have to be the only one condemned to work for a company where they immediately became highly suspicious at the slightest shortcoming? Were all employees, every one of them, louts, was there not one of them who was faithful and devoted who would go so mad with pangs of conscience that he couldn't get out of bed if he didn't spend at least a couple of hours in the morning on company business? Was it really not enough to let one of the trainees make enquiries - assuming enquiries were even necessary - did the chief clerk have to come himself, and did they have to show the whole, innocent family that this was so suspicious that only the chief clerk could be trusted to have the wisdom to investigate it? And more because these thoughts had made him upset than through any proper decision, he swang himself with all his force out of the bed. There was a loud thump, but it wasn't really a loud noise. His fall was softened a little by the carpet, and Gregor's back was also more elastic than he had thought, which made the sound muffled and not too noticeable. He had not held his head carefully enough, though, and hit it as he fell; annoyed and in pain, he turned it and rubbed it against the carpet.

"Something's fallen down in there", said the chief clerk in the room on the left. Gregor tried to imagine whether something of the sort that had happened to him today could ever happen to the chief clerk too; you had to concede that it was possible. But as if in gruff reply to this question, the chief clerk's firm footsteps in his highly polished boots could now be heard in the adjoining room. From the room on his right, Gregor's sister whispered to him to let him know: "Gregor, the chief clerk is here." "Yes, I know", said Gregor to himself; but without daring to raise his voice loud enough for his sister to hear him.

"Gregor", said his father now from the room to his left, "the chief clerk has come round and wants to know why you didn't leave on the early train. We don't know what to say to him. And anyway, he wants to speak to you personally. So please open up this door. I'm sure he'll be good enough to forgive the untidiness of your room." Then the chief clerk called "Good morning, Mr. Samsa". "He isn't well", said his mother to the chief clerk, while his father continued to speak through the door. "He isn't well, please believe me. Why else would Gregor have missed a train! The lad only ever thinks about the business. It nearly makes me cross the way he never goes out in the evenings; he's been in town for a week now but stayed home every evening. He sits with us in the kitchen and just reads the paper or studies train timetables. His idea of relaxation is working with his fretsaw. He's made a little frame, for instance, it only took him two or three evenings, you'll be amazed how nice it is; it's hanging up in his room; you'll see it as soon as Gregor opens the door. Anyway, I'm glad you're here; we wouldn't have been able to get Gregor to open the door by ourselves; he's so stubborn; and I'm sure he isn't well, he said this morning that he is, but he isn't." "I'll be there in a moment", said Gregor slowly and thoughtfully, but without moving so that he would not miss any word of the conversation. "Well I can't think of any other way of explaining it, Mrs. Samsa", said the chief clerk, "I hope it's nothing serious. But on the other hand, I must say that if we people in commerce ever become slightly unwell then, fortunately or unfortunately as you like, we simply have to overcome it because of business considerations." "Can the chief clerk come in to see you now then?", asked his father impatiently, knocking at the door again. "No", said Gregor. In the room on his right there followed a painful silence; in the room on his left his sister began to cry.

So why did his sister not go and join the others? She had probably only just got up and had not even begun to get dressed. And why was she crying? Was it because he had not got up, and had not let the chief clerk in, because he was in danger of losing his job and if that happened his boss would once more pursue their parents with the same demands as before? There was no need to worry about things like that yet. Gregor was still there and had not the slightest intention of abandoning his family. For the time being he just lay there on the carpet, and no-one who knew the condition he was in would seriously have expected him to let the chief clerk in. It was only a minor discourtesy, and a suitable excuse could easily be found for it later on, it was not something for which Gregor could be sacked on the spot. And it seemed to Gregor much more sensible to leave him now in peace instead of disturbing him with talking at him and crying. But the others didn't know what was happening, they were worried, that would excuse their behaviour.

The chief clerk now raised his voice, "Mr. Samsa", he called to him, "what is wrong? You barricade yourself in your room, give us no more than yes or no for an answer, you are causing serious and unnecessary concern to your parents and you fail - and I mention this just by the way - you fail to carry out your business duties in a way that is quite unheard of. I'm speaking here on behalf of your parents and of your employer, and really must request a clear and immediate explanation. I am astonished, quite astonished. I thought I knew you as a calm and sensible person, and now you suddenly seem to be showing off with peculiar whims. This morning, your employer did suggest a possible reason for your failure to appear, it's true - it had to do with the money that was recently entrusted to you - but I came near to giving him my word of honour that that could not be the right explanation. But now that I see your incomprehensible stubbornness I no longer feel any wish whatsoever to intercede on your behalf. And nor is your position all that secure. I had originally intended to say all this to you in private, but since you cause me to waste my time here for no good reason I don't see why your parents should not also learn of it. Your turnover has been very unsatisfactory of late; I grant you that it's not the time of year to do especially good business, we recognise that; but there simply is no time of year to do no business at all, Mr. Samsa, we cannot allow there to be."

"But Sir", called Gregor, beside himself and forgetting all else in the excitement, "I'll open up immediately, just a moment. I'm slightly unwell, an attack of dizziness, I haven't been able to get up. I'm still in bed now. I'm quite fresh again now, though. I'm just getting out of bed. Just a moment. Be patient! It's not quite as easy as I'd thought. I'm quite alright now, though. It's shocking, what can suddenly happen to a person! I was quite alright last night, my parents know about it, perhaps better than me, I had a small symptom of it last night already. They must have noticed it.

I don't know why I didn't let you know at work! But you always think you can get over an illness without staying at home. Please, don't make my parents suffer! There's no basis for any of the accusations you're making; nobody's ever said a word to me about any of these things. Maybe you haven't read the latest contracts I sent in. I'll set off with the eight o'clock train, as well, these few hours of rest have given me strength. You don't need to wait, sir; I'll be in the office soon after you, and please be so good as to tell that to the boss and recommend me to him!"

And while Gregor gushed out these words, hardly knowing what he was saying, he made his way over to the chest of drawers - this was easily done, probably because of the practise he had already had in bed - where he now tried to get himself upright. He really did want to open the door, really did want to let them see him and to speak with the chief clerk; the others were being so insistent, and he was curious to learn what they would say when they caught sight of him. If they were shocked then it would no longer be Gregor's responsibility and he could rest. If, however, they took everything calmly he would still have no reason to be upset, and if he hurried he really could be at the station for eight o'clock. The first few times he tried to climb up on the smooth chest of drawers he just slid down again, but he finally gave himself one last swing and stood there upright; the lower part of his body was in serious pain but he no longer gave any attention to it. Now he let himself fall against the back of a nearby chair and held tightly to the edges of it with his little legs. By now he had also calmed down, and kept quiet so that he could listen to what the chief clerk was saying.

"Did you understand a word of all that?" the chief clerk asked his parents, "surely he's not trying to make fools of us". "Oh, God!" called his mother, who was already in tears, "he could be seriously ill and we're making him suffer. Grete! Grete!" she then cried. "Mother?" his sister called from the other side. They communicated across Gregor's room. "You'll have to go for the doctor straight away. Gregor is ill. Quick, get the doctor. Did you hear the way Gregor spoke just now?" "That was the voice of an animal", said the chief clerk, with a calmness that was in contrast with his mother's screams. "Anna! Anna!" his father called into the kitchen through the entrance hall, clapping his hands, "get a locksmith here, now!" And the two girls, their skirts swishing, immediately ran out through the hall, wrenching open the front door of the flat as they went. How had his sister managed to get dressed so quickly? There was no sound of the door banging shut again; they must have left it open; people often do in homes where something awful has happened.

Gregor, in contrast, had become much calmer. So they couldn't understand his words any more, although they seemed clear enough to him, clearer than before - perhaps his ears had become used to the sound. They had realised, though, that there was something wrong with him, and were ready to help. The first response to his situation had been confident and wise, and that made him feel better. He felt that he had been drawn back in among people, and from the doctor and the locksmith he expected great and surprising achievements - although he did not really distinguish one from the other. Whatever was said next would be crucial, so, in order to make his voice as clear as possible, he coughed a little, but taking care to do this not too loudly as even this might well sound different from the way that a human coughs and he was no longer sure he could judge this for himself. Meanwhile, it had become very quiet in the next room. Perhaps his parents were sat at the table whispering with the chief clerk, or perhaps they were all pressed against the door and listening.

Gregor slowly pushed his way over to the door with the chair. Once there he let go of it and threw himself onto the door, holding himself upright against it using the adhesive on the tips of his legs. He rested there a little while to recover from the effort involved and then set himself to the task of turning the key in the lock with his mouth. He seemed, unfortunately, to have no proper teeth - how was he, then, to grasp the key? - but the lack of teeth was, of course, made up for with a very strong jaw; using the jaw, he really was able to start the key turning, ignoring the fact that he must have been causing some kind of damage as a brown fluid came from his mouth, flowed over the key and dripped onto the floor. "Listen", said the chief clerk in the next room, "he's turning the key." Gregor was greatly encouraged by this; but they all should have been calling to him, his father and his mother too: "Well done, Gregor", they should have cried, "keep at it, keep hold of the lock!" And with the idea that they were all excitedly following his efforts, he bit on the key with all his strength, paying no attention to the pain he was causing himself. As the key turned round he turned around the lock with it, only holding himself upright with his mouth, and hung onto the key or pushed it down again with the whole weight of his body as needed. The clear sound of the lock as it snapped back was Gregor's sign that he could break his concentration, and as he regained his breath he said to himself: "So, I didn't need the locksmith after all". Then he lay his head on the handle of the door to open it completely.

Because he had to open the door in this way, it was already wide open before he could be seen. He had first to slowly turn himself around one of the double doors, and he had to do it very carefully if he did not want to fall flat on his back before entering the room. He was still occupied with this difficult movement, unable to pay attention to anything else, when he heard the chief clerk exclaim a loud "Oh!", which sounded like the soughing of the wind. Now he also saw him - he was the nearest to the door - his hand pressed against his open mouth and slowly retreating as if driven by a steady and invisible force. Gregor's mother, her hair still dishevelled from bed despite the chief clerk's being there, looked at his father. Then she unfolded her arms, took two steps forward towards Gregor and sank down onto the floor into her skirts that spread themselves out around her as her head disappeared down onto her breast. His father looked hostile, and clenched his fists as if wanting to knock Gregor back into his room. Then he looked uncertainly round the living room, covered his eyes with his hands and wept so that his powerful chest shook.

So Gregor did not go into the room, but leant against the inside of the other door which was still held bolted in place. In this way only half of his body could be seen, along with his head above it which he leant over to one side as he peered out at the others. Meanwhile the day had become much lighter; part of the endless, grey-black building on the other side of the street - which was a hospital - could be seen quite clearly with the austere and regular line of windows piercing its façade; the rain was still falling, now throwing down large, individual droplets which hit the ground one at a time. The washing up from breakfast lay on the table; there was so much of it because, for Gregor's father, breakfast was the most important meal of the day and he would stretch it out for several hours as he sat reading a number of different newspapers. On the wall exactly opposite there was photograph of Gregor when he was a lieutenant in the army, his sword in his hand and a carefree smile on his face as he called forth respect for his uniform and bearing. The door to the entrance hall was open and as the front door of the flat was also open he could see onto the landing and the stairs where they began their way down below.

"Now, then", said Gregor, well aware that he was the only one to have kept calm, "I'll get dressed straight away now, pack up my samples and set off. Will you please just let me leave? You can see", he said to the chief clerk, "that I'm not stubborn and I like to do my job; being a commercial traveller is arduous but without travelling I couldn't earn my living. So where are you going, in to the office? Yes? Will you report everything accurately, then? It's quite possible for someone to be temporarily unable to work, but that's just the right time to remember what's been achieved in the past and consider that later on, once the difficulty has been removed, he will certainly work with all the more diligence and concentration. You're well aware that I'm seriously in debt to our employer as well as having to look after my parents and my sister, so that I'm trapped in a difficult situation, but I will work my way out of it again. Please don't make things any harder for me than they are already, and don't take sides against me at the office. I know that nobody likes the travellers. They think we earn an enormous wage as well as having a soft time of it. That's just prejudice but they have no particular reason to think better of it. But you, sir, you have a better overview than the rest of the staff, in fact, if I can say this in confidence, a better overview than the boss himself - it's very easy for a businessman like him to make mistakes about his employees and judge them more harshly than he should. And you're also well aware that we travellers spend almost the whole year away from the office, so that we can very easily fall victim to gossip and chance and groundless complaints, and it's almost impossible to defend yourself from that sort of thing, we don't usually even hear about them, or if at all it's when we arrive back home exhausted from a trip, and that's when we feel the harmful effects of what's been going on without even knowing what caused them. Please, don't go away, at least first say something to show that you grant that I'm at least partly right!"

But the chief clerk had turned away as soon as Gregor had started to speak, and, with protruding lips, only stared back at him over his trembling shoulders as he left. He did not keep still for a moment while Gregor was speaking, but moved steadily towards the door without taking his eyes off him. He moved very gradually, as if there had been some secret prohibition on leaving the room. It was only when he had reached the entrance hall that he made a sudden movement, drew his foot from the living room, and rushed forward in a panic. In the hall, he stretched his right hand far out towards the stairway as if out there, there were some supernatural force waiting to save him.

Gregor realised that it was out of the question to let the chief clerk go away in this mood if his position in the firm was not to be put into extreme danger. That was something his parents did not understand very well; over the years, they had become convinced that this job would provide for Gregor for his entire life, and besides, they had so much to worry about at present that they had lost sight of any thought for the future. Gregor, though, did think about the future. The chief clerk had to be held back, calmed down, convinced and finally won over; the future of Gregor and his family depended on it! If only his sister were here! She was clever; she was already in tears while Gregor was still lying peacefully on his back. And the chief clerk was a lover of women, surely she could persuade him; she would close the front door in the entrance hall and talk him out of his shocked state. But his sister was not there, Gregor would have to do the job himself. And without considering that he still was not familiar with how well he could move about in his present state, or that his speech still might not - or probably would not - be understood, he let go of the door; pushed himself through the opening; tried to reach the chief clerk on the landing who, ridiculously, was holding on to the banister with both hands; but Gregor fell immediately over and, with a little scream as he sought something to hold onto, landed on his numerous little legs. Hardly had that happened than, for the first time that day, he began to feel alright with his body; the little legs had the solid ground under them; to his pleasure, they did exactly as he told them; they were even making the effort to carry him where he wanted to go; and he was soon believing that all his sorrows would soon be finally at an end. He held back the urge to move but swayed from side to side as he crouched there on the floor. His mother was not far away in front of him and seemed, at first, quite engrossed in herself, but then she suddenly jumped up with her arms outstretched and her fingers spread shouting: "Help, for pity's sake, Help!" The way she held her head suggested she wanted to see Gregor better, but the unthinking way she was hurrying backwards showed that she did not; she had forgotten that the table was behind her with all the breakfast things on it; when she reached the table she sat quickly down on it without knowing what she was doing; without even seeming to notice that the coffee pot had been knocked over and a gush of coffee was pouring down onto the carpet.

"Mother, mother", said Gregor gently, looking up at her. He had completely forgotten the chief clerk for the moment, but could not help himself snapping in the air with his jaws at the sight of the flow of coffee. That set his mother screaming anew, she fled from the table and into the arms of his father as he rushed towards her. Gregor, though, had no time to spare for his parents now; the chief clerk had already reached the stairs; with his chin on the banister, he looked back for the last time. Gregor made a run for him; he wanted to be sure of reaching him; the chief clerk must have expected something, as he leapt down several steps at once and disappeared; his shouts resounding all around the staircase. The flight of the chief clerk seemed, unfortunately, to put Gregor's father into a panic as well. Until then he had been relatively self controlled, but now, instead of running after the chief clerk himself, or at least not impeding Gregor as he ran after him, Gregor's father seized the chief clerk's stick in his right hand (the chief clerk had left it behind on a chair, along with his hat and overcoat), picked up a large newspaper from the table with his left, and used them to drive Gregor back into his room, stamping his foot at him as he went. Gregor's appeals to his father were of no help, his appeals were simply not understood, however much he humbly turned his head his father merely stamped his foot all the harder. Across the room, despite the chilly weather, Gregor's mother had pulled open a window, leant far out of it and pressed her hands to her face. A strong draught of air flew in from the street towards the stairway, the curtains flew up, the newspapers on the table fluttered and some of them were blown onto the floor. Nothing would stop Gregor's father as he drove him back, making hissing noises at him like a wild man. Gregor had never had any practice in moving backwards and was only able to go very slowly. If Gregor had only been allowed to turn round he would have been back in his room straight away, but he was afraid that if he took the time to do that his father would become impatient, and there was the threat of a lethal blow to his back or head from the stick in his father's hand any moment. Eventually, though, Gregor realised that he had no choice as he saw, to his disgust, that he was quite incapable of going backwards in a straight line; so he began, as quickly as possible and with frequent anxious glances at his father, to turn himself round. It went very slowly, but perhaps his father was able to see his good intentions as he did nothing to hinder him, in fact now and then he used the tip of his stick to give directions from a distance as to which way to turn. If only his father would stop that unbearable hissing! It was making Gregor quite confused. When he had nearly finished turning round, still listening to that hissing, he made a mistake and turned himself back a little the way he had just come. He was pleased when he finally had his head in front of the doorway, but then saw that it was too narrow, and his body was too broad to get through it without further difficulty. In his present mood, it obviously did not occur to his father to open the other of the double doors so that Gregor would have enough space to get through. He was merely fixed on the idea that Gregor should be got back into his room as quickly as possible. Nor would he ever have allowed Gregor the time to get himself upright as preparation for getting through the doorway. What he did, making more noise than ever, was to drive Gregor forwards all the harder as if there had been nothing in the way; it sounded to Gregor as if there was now more than one father behind him; it was not a pleasant experience, and Gregor pushed himself into the doorway without regard for what might happen. One side of his body lifted itself, he lay at an angle in the doorway, one flank scraped on the white door and was painfully injured, leaving vile brown flecks on it, soon he was stuck fast and would not have been able to move at all by himself, the little legs along one side hung quivering in the air while those on the other side were pressed painfully against the ground. Then his father gave him a hefty shove from behind which released him from where he was held and sent him flying, and heavily bleeding, deep into his room. The door was slammed shut with the stick, then, finally, all was quiet.

II

It was not until it was getting dark that evening that Gregor awoke from his deep and coma-like sleep. He would have woken soon afterwards anyway even if he hadn't been disturbed, as he had had enough sleep and felt fully rested. But he had the impression that some hurried steps and the sound of the door leading into the front room being carefully shut had woken him. The light from the electric street lamps shone palely here and there onto the ceiling and tops of the furniture, but down below, where Gregor was, it was dark. He pushed himself over to the door, feeling his way clumsily with his antennae - of which he was now beginning to learn the value - in order to see what had been happening there. The whole of his left side seemed like one, painfully stretched scar, and he limped badly on his two rows of legs. One of the legs had been badly injured in the events of that morning - it was nearly a miracle that only one of them had been - and dragged along lifelessly.

It was only when he had reached the door that he realised what it actually was that had drawn him over to it; it was the smell of something to eat. By the door there was a dish filled with sweetened milk with little pieces of white bread floating in it. He was so pleased he almost laughed, as he was even hungrier than he had been that morning, and immediately dipped his head into the milk, nearly covering his eyes with it. But he soon drew his head back again in disappointment; not only did the pain in his tender left side make it difficult to eat the food - he was only able to eat if his whole body worked together as a snuffling whole - but the milk did not taste at all nice. Milk like this was normally his favourite drink, and his sister had certainly left it there for him because of that, but he turned, almost against his own will, away from the dish and crawled back into the centre of the room.

Through the crack in the door, Gregor could see that the gas had been lit in the living room. His father at this time would normally be sat with his evening paper, reading it out in a loud voice to Gregor's mother, and sometimes to his sister, but there was now not a sound to be heard. Gregor's sister would often write and tell him about this reading, but maybe his father had lost the habit in recent times. It was so quiet all around too, even though there must have been somebody in the flat. "What a quiet life it is the family lead", said Gregor to himself, and, gazing into the darkness, felt a great pride that he was able to provide a life like that in such a nice home for his sister and parents. But what now, if all this peace and wealth and comfort should come to a horrible and frightening end? That was something that Gregor did not want to think about too much, so he started to move about, crawling up and down the room.

Once during that long evening, the door on one side of the room was opened very slightly and hurriedly closed again; later on the door on the other side did the same; it seemed that someone needed to enter the room but thought better of it. Gregor went and waited immediately by the door, resolved either to bring the timorous visitor into the room in some way or at least to find out who it was; but the door was opened no more that night and Gregor waited in vain. The previous morning while the doors were locked everyone had wanted to get in there to him, but now, now that he had opened up one of the doors and the other had clearly been unlocked some time during the day, no-one came, and the keys were in the other sides.

It was not until late at night that the gaslight in the living room was put out, and now it was easy to see that his parents and sister had stayed awake all that time, as they all could be distinctly heard as they went away together on tip-toe. It was clear that no-one would come into Gregor's room any more until morning; that gave him plenty of time to think undisturbed about how he would have to re-arrange his life. For some reason, the tall, empty room where he was forced to remain made him feel uneasy as he lay there flat on the floor, even though he had been living in it for five years. Hardly aware of what he was doing other than a slight feeling of shame, he hurried under the couch. It pressed down on his back a little, and he was no longer able to lift his head, but he nonetheless felt immediately at ease and his only regret was that his body was too broad to get it all underneath.

He spent the whole night there. Some of the time he passed in a light sleep, although he frequently woke from it in alarm because of his hunger, and some of the time was spent in worries and vague hopes which, however, always led to the same conclusion: for the time being he must remain calm, he must show patience and the greatest consideration so that his family could bear the unpleasantness that he, in his present condition, was forced to impose on them.

Gregor soon had the opportunity to test the strength of his decisions, as early the next morning, almost before the night had ended, his sister, nearly fully dressed, opened the door from the front room and looked anxiously in. She did not see him straight away, but when she did notice him under the couch - he had to be somewhere, for God's sake, he couldn't have flown away - she was so shocked that she lost control of herself and slammed the door shut again from outside. But she seemed to regret her behaviour, as she opened the door again straight away and came in on tip-toe as if entering the room of someone seriously ill or even of a stranger. Gregor had pushed his head forward, right to the edge of the couch, and watched her. Would she notice that he had left the milk as it was, realise that it was not from any lack of hunger and bring him in some other food that was more suitable? If she didn't do it herself he would rather go hungry than draw her attention to it, although he did feel a terrible urge to rush forward from under the couch, throw himself at his sister's feet and beg her for something good to eat. However, his sister noticed the full dish immediately and looked at it and the few drops of milk splashed around it with some surprise. She immediately picked it up - using a rag, not her bare hands - and carried it out. Gregor was extremely curious as to what she would bring in its place, imagining the wildest possibilities, but he never could have guessed what his sister, in her goodness, actually did bring. In order to test his taste, she brought him a whole selection of things, all spread out on an old newspaper. There were old, half-rotten vegetables; bones from the evening meal, covered in white sauce that had gone hard; a few raisins and almonds; some cheese that Gregor had declared inedible two days before; a dry roll and some bread spread with butter and salt. As well as all that she had poured some water into the dish, which had probably been permanently set aside for Gregor's use, and placed it beside them. Then, out of consideration for Gregor's feelings, as she knew that he would not eat in front of her, she hurried out again and even turned the key in the lock so that Gregor would know he could make things as comfortable for himself as he liked. Gregor's little legs whirred, at last he could eat. What's more, his injuries must already have completely healed as he found no difficulty in moving. This amazed him, as more than a month earlier he had cut his finger slightly with a knife, he thought of how his finger had still hurt the day before yesterday. "Am I less sensitive than I used to be, then?", he thought, and was already sucking greedily at the cheese which had immediately, almost compellingly, attracted him much more than the other foods on the newspaper. Quickly one after another, his eyes watering with pleasure, he consumed the cheese, the vegetables and the sauce; the fresh foods, on the other hand, he didn't like at all, and even dragged the things he did want to eat a little way away from them because he couldn't stand the smell. Long after he had finished eating and lay lethargic in the same place, his sister slowly turned the key in the lock as a sign to him that he should withdraw. He was immediately startled, although he had been half asleep, and he hurried back under the couch. But he needed great self-control to stay there even for the short time that his sister was in the room, as eating so much food had rounded out his body a little and he could hardly breathe in that narrow space. Half suffocating, he watched with bulging eyes as his sister unselfconsciously took a broom and swept up the left-overs, mixing them in with the food he had not even touched at all as if it could not be used any more. She quickly dropped it all into a bin, closed it with its wooden lid, and carried everything out. She had hardly turned her back before Gregor came out again from under the couch and stretched himself.

This was how Gregor received his food each day now, once in the morning while his parents and the maid were still asleep, and the second time after everyone had eaten their meal at midday as his parents would sleep for a little while then as well, and Gregor's sister would send the maid away on some errand. Gregor's father and mother certainly did not want him to starve either, but perhaps it would have been more than they could stand to have any more experience of his feeding than being told about it, and perhaps his sister wanted to spare them what distress she could as they were indeed suffering enough.

It was impossible for Gregor to find out what they had told the doctor and the locksmith that first morning to get them out of the flat. As nobody could understand him, nobody, not even his sister, thought that he could understand them, so he had to be content to hear his sister's sighs and appeals to the saints as she moved about his room. It was only later, when she had become a little more used to everything - there was, of course, no question of her ever becoming fully used to the situation - that Gregor would sometimes catch a friendly comment, or at least a comment that could be construed as friendly. "He's enjoyed his dinner today", she might say when he had diligently cleared away all the food left for him, or if he left most of it, which slowly became more and more frequent, she would often say, sadly, "now everything's just been left there again".

Although Gregor wasn't able to hear any news directly he did listen to much of what was said in the next rooms, and whenever he heard anyone speaking he would scurry straight to the appropriate door and press his whole body against it. There was seldom any conversation, especially at first, that was not about him in some way, even if only in secret. For two whole days, all the talk at every mealtime was about what they should do now; but even between meals they spoke about the same subject as there were always at least two members of the family at home - nobody wanted to be at home by themselves and it was out of the question to leave the flat entirely empty. And on the very first day the maid had fallen to her knees and begged Gregor's mother to let her go without delay. It was not very clear how much she knew of what had happened but she left within a quarter of an hour, tearfully thanking Gregor's mother for her dismissal as if she had done her an enormous service. She even swore emphatically not to tell anyone the slightest about what had happened, even though no-one had asked that of her.

Now Gregor's sister also had to help his mother with the cooking; although that was not so much bother as no-one ate very much. Gregor often heard how one of them would unsuccessfully urge another to eat, and receive no more answer than "no thanks, I've had enough" or something similar. No-one drank very much either. His sister would sometimes ask his father whether he would like a beer, hoping for the chance to go and fetch it herself. When his father then said nothing she would add, so that he would not feel selfish, that she could send the housekeeper for it, but then his father would close the matter with a big, loud "No", and no more would be said.

Even before the first day had come to an end, his father had explained to Gregor's mother and sister what their finances and prospects were. Now and then he stood up from the table and took some receipt or document from the little cash box he had saved from his business when it had collapsed five years earlier. Gregor heard how he opened the complicated lock and then closed it again after he had taken the item he wanted. What he heard his father say was some of the first good news that Gregor heard since he had first been incarcerated in his room. He had thought that nothing at all remained from his father's business, at least he had never told him anything different, and Gregor had never asked him about it anyway. Their business misfortune had reduced the family to a state of total despair, and Gregor's only concern at that time had been to arrange things so that they could all forget about it as quickly as possible. So then he started working especially hard, with a fiery vigour that raised him from a junior salesman to a travelling representative almost overnight, bringing with it the chance to earn money in quite different ways. Gregor converted his success at work straight into cash that he could lay on the table at home for the benefit of his astonished and delighted family. They had been good times and they had never come again, at least not with the same splendour, even though Gregor had later earned so much that he was in a position to bear the costs of the whole family, and did bear them. They had even got used to it, both Gregor and the family, they took the money with gratitude and he was glad to provide it, although there was no longer much warm affection given in return. Gregor only remained close to his sister now. Unlike him, she was very fond of music and a gifted and expressive violinist, it was his secret plan to send her to the conservatory next year even though it would cause great expense that would have to be made up for in some other way. During Gregor's short periods in town, conversation with his sister would often turn to the conservatory but it was only ever mentioned as a lovely dream that could never be realised. Their parents did not like to hear this innocent talk, but Gregor thought about it quite hard and decided he would let them know what he planned with a grand announcement of it on Christmas day.

That was the sort of totally pointless thing that went through his mind in his present state, pressed upright against the door and listening. There were times when he simply became too tired to continue listening, when his head would fall wearily against the door and he would pull it up again with a start, as even the slightest noise he caused would be heard next door and they would all go silent. "What's that he's doing now", his father would say after a while, clearly having gone over to the door, and only then would the interrupted conversation slowly be taken up again.

When explaining things, his father repeated himself several times, partly because it was a long time since he had been occupied with these matters himself and partly because Gregor's mother did not understand everything the first time. From these repeated explanations Gregor learned, to his pleasure, that despite all their misfortunes there was still some money available from the old days. It was not a lot, but it had not been touched in the meantime and some interest had accumulated. Besides that, they had not been using up all the money that Gregor had been bringing home every month, keeping only a little for himself, so that that, too, had been accumulating. Behind the door, Gregor nodded with enthusiasm in his pleasure at this unexpected thrift and caution. He could actually have used this surplus money to reduce his father's debt to his boss, and the day when he could have freed himself from that job would have come much closer, but now it was certainly better the way his father had done things.

This money, however, was certainly not enough to enable the family to live off the interest; it was enough to maintain them for, perhaps, one or two years, no more. That's to say, it was money that should not really be touched but set aside for emergencies; money to live on had to be earned. His father was healthy but old, and lacking in self confidence. During the five years that he had not been working - the first holiday in a life that had been full of strain and no success - he had put on a lot of weight and become very slow and clumsy. Would Gregor's elderly mother now have to go and earn money? She suffered from asthma and it was a strain for her just to move about the home, every other day would be spent struggling for breath on the sofa by the open window. Would his sister have to go and earn money? She was still a child of seventeen, her life up till then had been very enviable, consisting of wearing nice clothes, sleeping late, helping out in the business, joining in with a few modest pleasures and most of all playing the violin. Whenever they began to talk of the need to earn money, Gregor would always first let go of the door and then throw himself onto the cool, leather sofa next to it, as he became quite hot with shame and regret.

He would often lie there the whole night through, not sleeping a wink but scratching at the leather for hours on end. Or he might go to all the effort of pushing a chair to the window, climbing up onto the sill and, propped up in the chair, leaning on the window to stare out of it. He had used to feel a great sense of freedom from doing this, but doing it now was obviously something more remembered than experienced, as what he actually saw in this way was becoming less distinct every day, even things that were quite near; he had used to curse the ever-present view of the hospital across the street, but now he could not see it at all, and if he had not known that he lived in Charlottenstrasse, which was a quiet street despite being in the middle of the city, he could have thought that he was looking out the window at a barren waste where the grey sky and the grey earth mingled inseparably. His observant sister only needed to notice the chair twice before she would always push it back to its exact position by the window after she had tidied up the room, and even left the inner pane of the window open from then on.

If Gregor had only been able to speak to his sister and thank her for all that she had to do for him it would have been easier for him to bear it; but as it was it caused him pain. His sister, naturally, tried as far as possible to pretend there was nothing burdensome about it, and the longer it went on, of course, the better she was able to do so, but as time went by Gregor was also able to see through it all so much better. It had even become very unpleasant for him, now, whenever she entered the room. No sooner had she come in than she would quickly close the door as a precaution so that no-one would have to suffer the view into Gregor's room, then she would go straight to the window and pull it hurriedly open almost as if she were suffocating. Even if it was cold, she would stay at the window breathing deeply for a little while. She would alarm Gregor twice a day with this running about and noise making; he would stay under the couch shivering the whole while, knowing full well that she would certainly have liked to spare him this ordeal, but it was impossible for her to be in the same room with him with the windows closed.

One day, about a month after Gregor's transformation when his sister no longer had any particular reason to be shocked at his appearance, she came into the room a little earlier than usual and found him still staring out the window, motionless, and just where he would be most horrible. In itself, his sister's not coming into the room would have been no surprise for Gregor as it would have been difficult for her to immediately open the window while he was still there, but not only did she not come in, she went straight back and closed the door behind her, a stranger would have thought he had threatened her and tried to bite her. Gregor went straight to hide himself under the couch, of course, but he had to wait until midday before his sister came back and she seemed much more uneasy than usual. It made him realise that she still found his appearance unbearable and would continue to do so, she probably even had to overcome the urge to flee when she saw the little bit of him that protruded from under the couch. One day, in order to spare her even this sight, he spent four hours carrying the bedsheet over to the couch on his back and arranged it so that he was completely covered and his sister would not be able to see him even if she bent down. If she did not think this sheet was necessary then all she had to do was take it off again, as it was clear enough that it was no pleasure for Gregor to cut himself off so completely. She left the sheet where it was. Gregor even thought he glimpsed a look of gratitude one time when he carefully looked out from under the sheet to see how his sister liked the new arrangement.

For the first fourteen days, Gregor's parents could not bring themselves to come into the room to see him. He would often hear them say how they appreciated all the new work his sister was doing even though, before, they had seen her as a girl who was somewhat useless and frequently been annoyed with her. But now the two of them, father and mother, would often both wait outside the door of Gregor's room while his sister tidied up in there, and as soon as she went out again she would have to tell them exactly how everything looked, what Gregor had eaten, how he had behaved this time and whether, perhaps, any slight improvement could be seen. His mother also wanted to go in and visit Gregor relatively soon but his father and sister at first persuaded her against it. Gregor listened very closely to all this, and approved fully. Later, though, she had to be held back by force, which made her call out: "Let me go and see Gregor, he is my unfortunate son! Can't you understand I have to see him?", and Gregor would think to himself that maybe it would be better if his mother came in, not every day of course, but one day a week, perhaps; she could understand everything much better than his sister who, for all her courage, was still just a child after all, and really might not have had an adult's appreciation of the burdensome job she had taken on.

Gregor's wish to see his mother was soon realised. Out of consideration for his parents, Gregor wanted to avoid being seen at the window during the day, the few square meters of the floor did not give him much room to crawl about, it was hard to just lie quietly through the night, his food soon stopped giving him any pleasure at all, and so, to entertain himself, he got into the habit of crawling up and down the walls and ceiling. He was especially fond of hanging from the ceiling; it was quite different from lying on the floor; he could breathe more freely; his body had a light swing to it; and up there, relaxed and almost happy, it might happen that he would surprise even himself by letting go of the ceiling and landing on the floor with a crash. But now, of course, he had far better control of his body than before and, even with a fall as great as that, caused himself no damage. Very soon his sister noticed Gregor's new way of entertaining himself - he had, after all, left traces of the adhesive from his feet as he crawled about - and got it into her head to make it as easy as possible for him by removing the furniture that got in his way, especially the chest of drawers and the desk. Now, this was not something that she would be able to do by herself; she did not dare to ask for help from her father; the sixteen year old maid had carried on bravely since the cook had left but she certainly would not have helped in this, she had even asked to be allowed to keep the kitchen locked at all times and never to have to open the door unless it was especially important; so his sister had no choice but to choose some time when Gregor's father was not there and fetch his mother to help her. As she approached the room, Gregor could hear his mother express her joy, but once at the door she went silent. First, of course, his sister came in and looked round to see that everything in the room was alright; and only then did she let her mother enter. Gregor had hurriedly pulled the sheet down lower over the couch and put more folds into it so that everything really looked as if it had just been thrown down by chance. Gregor also refrained, this time, from spying out from under the sheet; he gave up the chance to see his mother until later and was simply glad that she had come. "You can come in, he can't be seen", said his sister, obviously leading her in by the hand. The old chest of drawers was too heavy for a pair of feeble women to be heaving about, but Gregor listened as they pushed it from its place, his sister always taking on the heaviest part of the work for herself and ignoring her mother's warnings that she would strain herself. This lasted a very long time. After labouring at it for fifteen minutes or more his mother said it would be better to leave the chest where it was, for one thing it was too heavy for them to get the job finished before Gregor's father got home and leaving it in the middle of the room it would be in his way even more, and for another thing it wasn't even sure that taking the furniture away would really be any help to him. She thought just the opposite; the sight of the bare walls saddened her right to her heart; and why wouldn't Gregor feel the same way about it, he'd been used to this furniture in his room for a long time and it would make him feel abandoned to be in an empty room like that. Then, quietly, almost whispering as if wanting Gregor (whose whereabouts she did not know) to hear not even the tone of her voice, as she was convinced that he did not understand her words, she added "and by taking the furniture away, won't it seem like we're showing that we've given up all hope of improvement and we're abandoning him to cope for himself? I think it'd be best to leave the room exactly the way it was before so that when Gregor comes back to us again he'll find everything unchanged and he'll be able to forget the time in between all the easier".

Hearing these words from his mother made Gregor realise that the lack of any direct human communication, along with the monotonous life led by the family during these two months, must have made him confused - he could think of no other way of explaining to himself why he had seriously wanted his room emptied out. Had he really wanted to transform his room into a cave, a warm room fitted out with the nice furniture he had inherited? That would have let him crawl around unimpeded in any direction, but it would also have let him quickly forget his past when he had still been human. He had come very close to forgetting, and it had only been the voice of his mother, unheard for so long, that had shaken him out of it. Nothing should be removed; everything had to stay; he could not do without the good influence the furniture had on his condition; and if the furniture made it difficult for him to crawl about mindlessly that was not a loss but a great advantage.

His sister, unfortunately, did not agree; she had become used to the idea, not without reason, that she was Gregor's spokesman to his parents about the things that concerned him. This meant that his mother's advice now was sufficient reason for her to insist on removing not only the chest of drawers and the desk, as she had thought at first, but all the furniture apart from the all-important couch. It was more than childish perversity, of course, or the unexpected confidence she had recently acquired, that made her insist; she had indeed noticed that Gregor needed a lot of room to crawl about in, whereas the furniture, as far as anyone could see, was of no use to him at all. Girls of that age, though, do become enthusiastic about things and feel they must get their way whenever they can. Perhaps this was what tempted Grete to make Gregor's situation seem even more shocking than it was so that she could do even more for him. Grete would probably be the only one who would dare enter a room dominated by Gregor crawling about the bare walls by himself.

So she refused to let her mother dissuade her. Gregor's mother already looked uneasy in his room, she soon stopped speaking and helped Gregor's sister to get the chest of drawers out with what strength she had. The chest of drawers was something that Gregor could do without if he had to, but the writing desk had to stay. Hardly had the two women pushed the chest of drawers, groaning, out of the room than Gregor poked his head out from under the couch to see what he could do about it. He meant to be as careful and considerate as he could, but, unfortunately, it was his mother who came back first while Grete in the next room had her arms round the chest, pushing and pulling at it from side to side by herself without, of course, moving it an inch. His mother was not used to the sight of Gregor, he might have made her ill, so Gregor hurried backwards to the far end of the couch. In his startlement, though, he was not able to prevent the sheet at its front from moving a little. It was enough to attract his mother's attention. She stood very still, remained there a moment, and then went back out to Grete.

Gregor kept trying to assure himself that nothing unusual was happening, it was just a few pieces of furniture being moved after all, but he soon had to admit that the women going to and fro, their little calls to each other, the scraping of the furniture on the floor, all these things made him feel as if he were being assailed from all sides. With his head and legs pulled in against him and his body pressed to the floor, he was forced to admit to himself that he could not stand all of this much longer. They were emptying his room out; taking away everything that was dear to him; they had already taken out the chest containing his fretsaw and other tools; now they threatened to remove the writing desk with its place clearly worn into the floor, the desk where he had done his homework as a business trainee, at high school, even while he had been at infant school - he really could not wait any longer to see whether the two women's intentions were good. He had nearly forgotten they were there anyway, as they were now too tired to say anything while they worked and he could only hear their feet as they stepped heavily on the floor.

So, while the women were leant against the desk in the other room catching their breath, he sallied out, changed direction four times not knowing what he should save first before his attention was suddenly caught by the picture on the wall - which was already denuded of everything else that had been on it - of the lady dressed in copious fur. He hurried up onto the picture and pressed himself against its glass, it held him firmly and felt good on his hot belly. This picture at least, now totally covered by Gregor, would certainly be taken away by no-one. He turned his head to face the door into the living room so that he could watch the women when they came back.

They had not allowed themselves a long rest and came back quite soon; Grete had put her arm around her mother and was nearly carrying her. "What shall we take now, then?", said Grete and looked around. Her eyes met those of Gregor on the wall. Perhaps only because her mother was there, she remained calm, bent her face to her so that she would not look round and said, albeit hurriedly and with a tremor in her voice: "Come on, let's go back in the living room for a while?" Gregor could see what Grete had in mind, she wanted to take her mother somewhere safe and then chase him down from the wall. Well, she could certainly try it! He sat unyielding on his picture. He would rather jump at Grete's face.

But Grete's words had made her mother quite worried, she stepped to one side, saw the enormous brown patch against the flowers of the wallpaper, and before she even realised it was Gregor that she saw screamed: "Oh God, oh God!" Arms outstretched, she fell onto the couch as if she had given up everything and stayed there immobile. "Gregor!" shouted his sister, glowering at him and shaking her fist. That was the first word she had spoken to him directly since his transformation. She ran into the other room to fetch some kind of smelling salts to bring her mother out of her faint; Gregor wanted to help too - he could save his picture later, although he stuck fast to the glass and had to pull himself off by force; then he, too, ran into the next room as if he could advise his sister like in the old days; but he had to just stand behind her doing nothing; she was looking into various bottles, he startled her when she turned round; a bottle fell to the ground and broke; a splinter cut Gregor's face, some kind of caustic medicine splashed all over him; now, without delaying any longer, Grete took hold of all the bottles she could and ran with them in to her mother; she slammed the door shut with her foot. So now Gregor was shut out from his mother, who, because of him, might be near to death; he could not open the door if he did not want to chase his sister away, and she had to stay with his mother; there was nothing for him to do but wait; and, oppressed with anxiety and self-reproach, he began to crawl about, he crawled over everything, walls, furniture, ceiling, and finally in his confusion as the whole room began to spin around him he fell down into the middle of the dinner table.

He lay there for a while, numb and immobile, all around him it was quiet, maybe that was a good sign. Then there was someone at the door. The maid, of course, had locked herself in her kitchen so that Grete would have to go and answer it. His father had arrived home. "What's happened?" were his first words; Grete's appearance must have made everything clear to him. She answered him with subdued voice, and openly pressed her face into his chest: "Mother's fainted, but she's better now. Gregor got out." "Just as I expected", said his father, "just as I always said, but you women wouldn't listen, would you." It was clear to Gregor that Grete had not said enough and that his father took it to mean that something bad had happened, that he was responsible for some act of violence. That meant Gregor would now have to try to calm his father, as he did not have the time to explain things to him even if that had been possible. So he fled to the door of his room and pressed himself against it so that his father, when he came in from the hall, could see straight away that Gregor had the best intentions and would go back into his room without delay, that it would not be necessary to drive him back but that they had only to open the door and he would disappear.

His father, though, was not in the mood to notice subtleties like that; "Ah!", he shouted as he came in, sounding as if he were both angry and glad at the same time. Gregor drew his head back from the door and lifted it towards his father. He really had not imagined his father the way he stood there now; of late, with his new habit of crawling about, he had neglected to pay attention to what was going on the rest of the flat the way he had done before. He really ought to have expected things to have changed, but still, still, was that really his father? The same tired man as used to be laying there entombed in his bed when Gregor came back from his business trips, who would receive him sitting in the armchair in his nightgown when he came back in the evenings; who was hardly even able to stand up but, as a sign of his pleasure, would just raise his arms and who, on the couple of times a year when they went for a walk together on a Sunday or public holiday wrapped up tightly in his overcoat between Gregor and his mother, would always labour his way forward a little more slowly than them, who were already walking slowly for his sake; who would place his stick down carefully and, if he wanted to say something would invariably stop and gather his companions around him. He was standing up straight enough now; dressed in a smart blue uniform with gold buttons, the sort worn by the employees at the banking institute; above the high, stiff collar of the coat his strong double-chin emerged; under the bushy eyebrows, his piercing, dark eyes looked out fresh and alert; his normally unkempt white hair was combed down painfully close to his scalp. He took his cap, with its gold monogram from, probably, some bank, and threw it in an arc right across the room onto the sofa, put his hands in his trouser pockets, pushing back the bottom of his long uniform coat, and, with look of determination, walked towards Gregor. He probably did not even know himself what he had in mind, but nonetheless lifted his feet unusually high. Gregor was amazed at the enormous size of the soles of his boots, but wasted no time with that - he knew full well, right from the first day of his new life, that his father thought it necessary to always be extremely strict with him. And so he ran up to his father, stopped when his father stopped, scurried forwards again when he moved, even slightly. In this way they went round the room several times without anything decisive happening, without even giving the impression of a chase as everything went so slowly. Gregor remained all this time on the floor, largely because he feared his father might see it as especially provoking if he fled onto the wall or ceiling. Whatever he did, Gregor had to admit that he certainly would not be able to keep up this running about for long, as for each step his father took he had to carry out countless movements. He became noticeably short of breath, even in his earlier life his lungs had not been very reliable. Now, as he lurched about in his efforts to muster all the strength he could for running he could hardly keep his eyes open; his thoughts became too slow for him to think of any other way of saving himself than running; he almost forgot that the walls were there for him to use although, here, they were concealed behind carefully carved furniture full of notches and protrusions - then, right beside him, lightly tossed, something flew down and rolled in front of him. It was an apple; then another one immediately flew at him; Gregor froze in shock; there was no longer any point in running as his father had decided to bombard him. He had filled his pockets with fruit from the bowl on the sideboard and now, without even taking the time for careful aim, threw one apple after another. These little, red apples rolled about on the floor, knocking into each other as if they had electric motors. An apple thrown without much force glanced against Gregor's back and slid off without doing any harm. Another one however, immediately following it, hit squarely and lodged in his back; Gregor wanted to drag himself away, as if he could remove the surprising, the incredible pain by changing his position; but he felt as if nailed to the spot and spread himself out, all his senses in confusion. The last thing he saw was the door of his room being pulled open, his sister was screaming, his mother ran out in front of her in her blouse (as his sister had taken off some of her clothes after she had fainted to make it easier for her to breathe), she ran to his father, her skirts unfastened and sliding one after another to the ground, stumbling over the skirts she pushed herself to his father, her arms around him, uniting herself with him totally - now Gregor lost his ability to see anything - her hands behind his father's head begging him to spare Gregor's life.

III

No-one dared to remove the apple lodged in Gregor's flesh, so it remained there as a visible reminder of his injury. He had suffered it there for more than a month, and his condition seemed serious enough to remind even his father that Gregor, despite his current sad and revolting form, was a family member who could not be treated as an enemy. On the contrary, as a family there was a duty to swallow any revulsion for him and to be patient, just to be patient.

Because of his injuries, Gregor had lost much of his mobility - probably permanently. He had been reduced to the condition of an ancient invalid and it took him long, long minutes to crawl across his room - crawling over the ceiling was out of the question - but this deterioration in his condition was fully (in his opinion) made up for by the door to the living room being left open every evening. He got into the habit of closely watching it for one or two hours before it was opened and then, lying in the darkness of his room where he could not be seen from the living room, he could watch the family in the light of the dinner table and listen to their conversation - with everyone's permission, in a way, and thus quite differently from before.

They no longer held the lively conversations of earlier times, of course, the ones that Gregor always thought about with longing when he was tired and getting into the damp bed in some small hotel room. All of them were usually very quiet nowadays. Soon after dinner, his father would go to sleep in his chair; his mother and sister would urge each other to be quiet; his mother, bent deeply under the lamp, would sew fancy underwear for a fashion shop; his sister, who had taken a sales job, learned shorthand and French in the evenings so that she might be able to get a better position later on. Sometimes his father would wake up and say to Gregor's mother "you're doing so much sewing again today!", as if he did not know that he had been dozing

- and then he would go back to sleep again while mother and sister would exchange a tired grin.

With a kind of stubbornness, Gregor's father refused to take his uniform off even at home; while his nightgown hung unused on its peg Gregor's father would slumber where he was, fully dressed, as if always ready to serve and expecting to hear the voice of his superior even here. The uniform had not been new to start with, but as a result of this it slowly became even shabbier despite the efforts of Gregor's mother and sister to look after it. Gregor would often spend the whole evening looking at all the stains on this coat, with its gold buttons always kept polished and shiny, while the old man in it would sleep, highly uncomfortable but peaceful.

As soon as it struck ten, Gregor's mother would speak gently to his father to wake him and try to persuade him to go to bed, as he couldn't sleep properly where he was and he really had to get his sleep if he was to be up at six to get to work. But since he had been in work he had become more obstinate and would always insist on staying longer at the table, even though he regularly fell asleep and it was then harder than ever to persuade him to exchange the chair for his bed. Then, however much mother and sister would importune him with little reproaches and warnings he would keep slowly shaking his head for a quarter of an hour with his eyes closed and refusing to get up. Gregor's mother would tug at his sleeve, whisper endearments into his ear, Gregor's sister would leave her work to help her mother, but nothing would have any effect on him. He would just sink deeper into his chair. Only when the two women took him under the arms he would abruptly open his eyes, look at them one after the other and say: "What a life! This is what peace I get in my old age!" And supported by the two women he would lift himself up carefully as if he were carrying the greatest load himself, let the women take him to the door, send them off and carry on by himself while

Gregor's mother would throw down her needle and his sister her pen so that they could run after his father and continue being of help to him.

Who, in this tired and overworked family, would have had time to give more attention to Gregor than was absolutely necessary? The household budget became even smaller; so now the maid was dismissed; an enormous, thick-boned charwoman with white hair that flapped around her head came every morning and evening to do the heaviest work; everything else was looked after by Gregor's mother on top of the large amount of sewing work she did. Gregor even learned, listening to the evening conversation about what price they had hoped for, that several items of jewellery belonging to the family had been sold, even though both mother and sister had been very fond of wearing them at functions and celebrations. But the loudest complaint was that although the flat was much too big for their present circumstances, they could not move out of it, there was no imaginable way of transferring Gregor to the new address. He could see quite well, though, that there were more reasons than consideration for him that made it difficult for them to move, it would have been quite easy to transport him in any suitable crate with a few air holes in it; the main thing holding the family back from their decision to move was much more to do with their total despair, and the thought that they had been struck with a misfortune unlike anything experienced by anyone else they knew or were related to. They carried out absolutely everything that the world expects from poor people, Gregor's father brought bank employees their breakfast, his mother sacrificed herself by washing clothes for strangers, his sister ran back and forth behind her desk at the behest of the customers, but they just did not have the strength to do any more. And the injury in Gregor's back began to hurt as much as when it was new. After they had come back from taking his father to bed Gregor's mother and sister would now leave their work where it was and sit close together, cheek to cheek; his mother would point to Gregor's room and say "Close that door, Grete", and then, when he was in the dark again, they would sit in the next room and their tears would mingle, or they would simply sit there staring dry-eyed at the table.

Gregor hardly slept at all, either night or day. Sometimes he would think of taking over the family's affairs, just like before, the next time the door was opened; he had long forgotten about his boss and the chief clerk, but they would appear again in his thoughts, the salesmen and the apprentices, that stupid teaboy, two or three friends from other businesses, one of the chambermaids from a provincial hotel, a tender memory that appeared and disappeared again, a cashier from a hat shop for whom his attention had been serious but too slow, - all of them appeared to him, mixed together with strangers and others he had forgotten, but instead of helping him and his family they were all of them inaccessible, and he was glad when they disappeared. Other times he was not at all in the mood to look after his family, he was filled with simple rage about the lack of attention he was shown, and although he could think of nothing he would have wanted, he made plans of how he could get into the pantry where he could take all the things he was entitled to, even if he was not hungry. Gregor's sister no longer thought about how she could please him but would hurriedly push some food or other into his room with her foot before she rushed out to work in the morning and at midday, and in the evening she would sweep it away again with the broom, indifferent as to whether it had been eaten or - more often than not - had been left totally untouched. She still cleared up the room in the evening, but now she could not have been any quicker about it. Smears of dirt were left on the walls, here and there were little balls of dust and filth. At first, Gregor went into one of the worst of these places when his sister arrived as a reproach to her, but he could have stayed there for weeks without his sister doing anything about it; she could see the dirt as well as he could but she had simply decided to leave him to it. At the same time she became touchy in a way that was quite new for her and which everyone in the family understood - cleaning up Gregor's room was for her and her alone. Gregor's mother did once thoroughly clean his room, and needed to use several bucketfuls of water to do it - although that much dampness also made Gregor ill and he lay flat on the couch, bitter and immobile. But his mother was to be punished still more for what she had done, as hardly had his sister arrived home in the evening than she noticed the change in Gregor's room and, highly aggrieved, ran back into the living room where, despite her mothers raised and imploring hands, she broke into convulsive tears. Her father, of course, was startled out of his chair and the two parents looked on astonished and helpless; then they, too, became agitated; Gregor's father, standing to the right of his mother, accused her of not leaving the cleaning of Gregor's room to his sister; from her left, Gregor's sister screamed at her that she was never to clean Gregor's room again; while his mother tried to draw his father, who was beside himself with anger, into the bedroom; his sister, quaking with tears, thumped on the table with her small fists; and Gregor hissed in anger that no-one had even thought of closing the door to save him the sight of this and all its noise.

Gregor's sister was exhausted from going out to work, and looking after Gregor as she had done before was even more work for her, but even so his mother ought certainly not to have taken her place. Gregor, on the other hand, ought not to be neglected. Now, though, the charwoman was here. This elderly widow, with a robust bone structure that made her able to withstand the hardest of things in her long life, wasn't really repelled by Gregor. Just by chance one day, rather than any real curiosity, she opened the door to Gregor's room and found herself face to face with him. He was taken totally by surprise, no-one was chasing him but he began to rush to and fro while she just stood there in amazement with her hands crossed in front of her. From then on she never failed to open the door slightly every evening and morning and look briefly in on him. At first she would call to him as she did so with words that she probably considered friendly, such as "come on then, you old dung-beetle!", or "look at the old dung-beetle there!" Gregor never responded to being spoken to in that way, but just remained where he was without moving as if the door had never even been opened. If only they had told this charwoman to clean up his room every day instead of letting her disturb him for no reason whenever she felt like it! One day, early in the morning while a heavy rain struck the windowpanes, perhaps indicating that spring was coming, she began to speak to him in that way once again. Gregor was so resentful of it that he started to move toward her, he was slow and infirm, but it was like a kind of attack. Instead of being afraid, the charwoman just lifted up one of the chairs from near the door and stood there with her mouth open, clearly intending not to close her mouth until the chair in her hand had been slammed down into Gregor's back. "Aren't you coming any closer, then?", she asked when Gregor turned round again, and she calmly put the chair back in the corner.

Gregor had almost entirely stopped eating. Only if he happened to find himself next to the food that had been prepared for him he might take some of it into his mouth to play with it, leave it there a few hours and then, more often than not, spit it out again. At first he thought it was distress at the state of his room that stopped him eating, but he had soon got used to the changes made there. They had got into the habit of putting things into this room that they had no room for anywhere else, and there were now many such things as one of the rooms in the flat had been rented out to three gentlemen. These earnest gentlemen - all three of them had full beards, as Gregor learned peering through the crack in the door one day - were painfully insistent on things' being tidy. This meant not only in their own room but, since they had taken a room in this establishment, in the entire flat and especially in the kitchen. Unnecessary clutter was something they could not tolerate, especially if it was dirty. They had moreover brought most of their own furnishings and equipment with them. For this reason, many things had become superfluous which, although they could not be sold, the family did not wish to discard. All these things found their way into Gregor's room. The dustbins from the kitchen found their way in there too. The charwoman was always in a hurry, and anything she couldn't use for the time being she would just chuck in there. He, fortunately, would usually see no more than the object and the hand that held it. The woman most likely meant to fetch the things back out again when she had time and the opportunity, or to throw everything out in one go, but what actually happened was that they were left where they landed when they had first been thrown unless Gregor made his way through the junk and moved it somewhere else. At first he moved it because, with no other room free where he could crawl about, he was forced to, but later on he came to enjoy it although moving about in that way left him sad and tired to death, and he would remain immobile for hours afterwards.

The gentlemen who rented the room would sometimes take their evening meal at home in the living room that was used by everyone, and so the door to this room was often kept closed in the evening. But Gregor found it easy to give up having the door open, he had, after all, often failed to make use of it when it was open and, without the family having noticed it, lain in his room in its darkest corner. One time, though, the charwoman left the door to the living room slightly open, and it remained open when the gentlemen who rented the room came in in the evening and the light was put on. They sat up at the table where, formerly, Gregor had taken his meals with his father and mother, they unfolded the serviettes and picked up their knives and forks. Gregor's mother immediately appeared in the doorway with a dish of meat and soon behind her came his sister with a dish piled high with potatoes. The food was steaming, and filled the room with its smell. The gentlemen bent over the dishes set in front of them as if they wanted to test the food before eating it, and the gentleman in the middle, who seemed to count as an authority for the other two, did indeed cut off a piece of meat while it was still in its dish, clearly wishing to establish whether it was sufficiently cooked or whether it should be sent back to the kitchen. It was to his satisfaction, and Gregor's mother and sister, who had been looking on anxiously, began to breathe again and smiled.

The family themselves ate in the kitchen. Nonetheless, Gregor's father came into the living room before he went into the kitchen, bowed once with his cap in his hand and did his round of the table. The gentlemen stood as one, and mumbled something into their beards. Then, once they were alone, they ate in near perfect silence. It seemed remarkable to Gregor that above all the various noises of eating their chewing teeth could still be heard, as if they had wanted to show Gregor that you need teeth in order to eat and it was not possible to perform anything with jaws that are toothless however nice they might be. "I'd like to eat something", said Gregor anxiously, "but not anything like they're eating. They do feed themselves. And here I am, dying!"

Throughout all this time, Gregor could not remember having heard the violin being played, but this evening it began to be heard from the kitchen. The three gentlemen had already finished their meal, the one in the middle had produced a newspaper, given a page to each of the others, and now they leant back in their chairs reading them and smoking. When the violin began playing they became attentive, stood up and went on tip-toe over to the door of the hallway where they stood pressed against each other. Someone must have heard them in the kitchen, as Gregor's father called out: "Is the playing perhaps unpleasant for the gentlemen? We can stop it straight away." "On the contrary", said the middle gentleman, "would the young lady not like to come in and play for us here in the room, where it is, after all, much more cosy and comfortable?" "Oh yes, we'd love to", called back Gregor's father as if he had been the violin player himself. The gentlemen stepped back into the room and waited. Gregor's father soon appeared with the music stand, his mother with the music and his sister with the violin. She calmly prepared everything for her to begin playing; his parents, who had never rented a room out before and therefore showed an exaggerated courtesy towards the three gentlemen, did not even dare to sit on their own chairs; his father leant against the door with his right hand pushed in between two buttons on his uniform coat; his mother, though, was offered a seat by one of the gentlemen and sat - leaving the chair where the gentleman happened to have placed it - out of the way in a corner.

His sister began to play; father and mother paid close attention, one on each side, to the movements of her hands. Drawn in by the playing, Gregor had dared to come forward a little and already had his head in the living room. Before, he had taken great pride in how considerate he was but now it hardly occurred to him that he had become so thoughtless about the others. What's more, there was now all the more reason to keep himself hidden as he was covered in the dust that lay everywhere in his room and flew up at the slightest movement; he carried threads, hairs, and remains of food about on his back and sides; he was much too indifferent to everything now to lay on his back and wipe himself on the carpet like he had used to do several times a day. And despite this condition, he was not too shy to move forward a little onto the immaculate floor of the living room.

No-one noticed him, though. The family was totally preoccupied with the violin playing; at first, the three gentlemen had put their hands in their pockets and come up far too close behind the music stand to look at all the notes being played, and they must have disturbed Gregor's sister, but soon, in contrast with the family, they withdrew back to the window with their heads sunk and talking to each other at half volume, and they stayed by the window while Gregor's father observed them anxiously. It really now seemed very obvious that they had expected to hear some beautiful or entertaining violin playing but had been disappointed, that they had had enough of the whole performance and it was only now out of politeness that they allowed their peace to be disturbed. It was especially unnerving, the way they all blew the smoke from their cigarettes upwards from their mouth and noses. Yet Gregor's sister was playing so beautifully. Her face was leant to one side, following the lines of music with a careful and melancholy expression. Gregor crawled a little further forward, keeping his head close to the ground so that he could meet her eyes if the chance came. Was he an animal if music could captivate him so? It seemed to him that he was being shown the way to the unknown nourishment he had been yearning for. He was determined to make his way forward to his sister and tug at her skirt to show her she might come into his room with her violin, as no-one appreciated her playing here as much as he would. He never wanted to let her out of his room, not while he lived, anyway; his shocking appearance should, for once, be of some use to him; he wanted to be at every door of his room at once to hiss and spit at the attackers; his sister should not be forced to stay with him, though, but stay of her own free will; she would sit beside him on the couch with her ear bent down to him while he told her how he had always intended to send her to the conservatory, how he would have told everyone about it last Christmas - had Christmas really come and gone already? - if this misfortune hadn't got in the way, and refuse to let anyone dissuade him from it. On hearing all this, his sister would break out in tears of emotion, and Gregor would climb up to her shoulder and kiss her neck, which, since she had been going out to work, she had kept free without any necklace or collar.

"Mr. Samsa!", shouted the middle gentleman to Gregor's father, pointing, without wasting any more words, with his forefinger at Gregor as he slowly moved forward. The violin went silent, the middle of the three gentlemen first smiled at his two friends, shaking his head, and then looked back at Gregor. His father seemed to think it more important to calm the three gentlemen before driving Gregor out, even though they were not at all upset and seemed to think Gregor was more entertaining than the violin playing had been. He rushed up to them with his arms spread out and attempted to drive them back into their room at the same time as trying to block their view of Gregor with his body. Now they did become a little annoyed, and it was not clear whether it was his father's behaviour that annoyed them or the dawning realisation that they had had a neighbour like Gregor in the next room without knowing it. They asked Gregor's father for explanations, raised their arms like he had, tugged excitedly at their beards and moved back towards their room only very slowly. Meanwhile Gregor's sister had overcome the despair she had fallen into when her playing was suddenly interrupted. She had let her hands drop and let violin and bow hang limply for a while but continued to look at the music as if still playing, but then she suddenly pulled herself together, lay the instrument on her mother's lap who still sat laboriously struggling for breath where she was, and ran into the next room which, under pressure from her father, the three gentlemen were more quickly moving toward. Under his sister's experienced hand, the pillows and covers on the beds flew up and were put into order and she had already finished making the beds and slipped out again before the three gentlemen had reached the room. Gregor's father seemed so obsessed with what he was doing that he forgot all the respect he owed to his tenants. He urged them and pressed them until, when he was already at the door of the room, the middle of the three gentlemen shouted like thunder and stamped his foot and thereby brought Gregor's father to a halt. "I declare here and now", he said, raising his hand and glancing at Gregor's mother and sister to gain their attention too, "that with regard to the repugnant conditions that prevail in this flat and with this family" - here he looked briefly but decisively at the floor - "I give immediate notice on my room. For the days that I have been living here I will, of course, pay nothing at all, on the contrary I will consider whether to proceed with some kind of action for damages from you, and believe me it would be very easy to set out the grounds for such an action." He was silent and looked straight ahead as if waiting for something. And indeed, his two friends joined in with the words: "And we also give immediate notice." With that, he took hold of the door handle and slammed the door.

Gregor's father staggered back to his seat, feeling his way with his hands, and fell into it; it looked as if he was stretching himself out for his usual evening nap but from the uncontrolled way his head kept nodding it could be seen that he was not sleeping at all. Throughout all this, Gregor had lain still where the three gentlemen had first seen him. His disappointment at the failure of his plan, and perhaps also because he was weak from hunger, made it impossible for him to move. He was sure that everyone would turn on him any moment, and he waited. He was not even startled out of this state when the violin on his mother's lap fell from her trembling fingers and landed loudly on the floor.

"Father, Mother", said his sister, hitting the table with her hand as introduction, "we can't carry on like this. Maybe you can't see it, but I can. I don't want to call this monster my brother, all I can say is: we have to try and get rid of it. We've done all that's humanly possible to look after it and be patient, I don't think anyone could accuse us of doing anything wrong."

"She's absolutely right", said Gregor's father to himself. His mother, who still had not had time to catch her breath, began to cough dully, her hand held out in front of her and a deranged expression in her eyes.

Gregor's sister rushed to his mother and put her hand on her forehead. Her words seemed to give Gregor's father some more definite ideas. He sat upright, played with his uniform cap between the plates left by the three gentlemen after their meal, and occasionally looked down at Gregor as he lay there immobile.

"We have to try and get rid of it", said Gregor's sister, now speaking only to her father, as her mother was too occupied with coughing to listen, "it'll be the death of both of you, I can see it coming. We can't all work as hard as we have to and then come home to be tortured like this, we can't endure it. I can't endure it any more." And she broke out so heavily in tears that they flowed down the face of her mother, and she wiped them away with mechanical hand movements.

"My child", said her father with sympathy and obvious understanding, "what are we to do?"

His sister just shrugged her shoulders as a sign of the helplessness and tears that had taken hold of her, displacing her earlier certainty.

"If he could just understand us", said his father almost as a question; his sister shook her hand vigorously through her tears as a sign that of that there was no question.

"If he could just understand us", repeated Gregor's father, closing his eyes in acceptance of his sister's certainty that

that was quite impossible, "then perhaps we could come to some kind of arrangement with him. But as it is ..."

"It's got to go", shouted his sister, "that's the only way, Father. You've got to get rid of the idea that that's Gregor. We've only harmed ourselves by believing it for so long. How can that be Gregor? If it were Gregor he would have seen long ago that it's not possible for human beings to live with an animal like that and he would have gone of his own free will. We wouldn't have a brother any more, then, but we could carry on with our lives and remember him with respect. As it is this animal is persecuting us, it's driven out our tenants, it obviously wants to take over the whole flat and force us to sleep on the streets. Father, look, just look", she suddenly screamed, "he's starting again!" In her alarm, which was totally beyond Gregor's comprehension, his sister even abandoned his mother as she pushed herself vigorously out of her chair as if more willing to sacrifice her own mother than stay anywhere near Gregor. She rushed over to behind her father, who had become excited merely because she was and stood up half raising his hands in front of Gregor's sister as if to protect her.

But Gregor had had no intention of frightening anyone, least of all his sister. All he had done was begin to turn round so that he could go back into his room, although that was in itself quite startling as his pain-wracked condition meant that turning round required a great deal of effort and he was using his head to help himself do it, repeatedly raising it and striking it against the floor. He stopped and looked round. They seemed to have realised his good intention and had only been alarmed briefly. Now they all looked at him in unhappy silence. His mother lay in her chair with her legs stretched out and pressed against each other, her eyes nearly closed with exhaustion; his sister sat next to his father with her arms around his neck.

"Maybe now they'll let me turn round", thought Gregor and went back to work. He could not help panting loudly with the effort and had sometimes to stop and take a rest. No-one was making him rush any more, everything was left up to him. As soon as he had finally finished turning round he began to move straight ahead. He was amazed at the great distance that separated him from his room, and could not understand how he had covered that distance in his weak state a little while before and almost without noticing it. He concentrated on crawling as fast as he could and hardly noticed that there was not a word, not any cry, from his family to distract him. He did not turn his head until he had reached the doorway. He did not turn it all the way round as he felt his neck becoming stiff, but it was nonetheless enough to see that nothing behind him had changed, only his sister had stood up. With his last glance he saw that his mother had now fallen completely asleep.

He was hardly inside his room before the door was hurriedly shut, bolted and locked. The sudden noise behind Gregor so startled him that his little legs collapsed under him. It was his sister who had been in so much of a rush. She had been standing there waiting and sprung forward lightly, Gregor had not heard her coming at all, and as she turned the key in the lock she said loudly to her parents "At last!".

"What now, then?", Gregor asked himself as he looked round in the darkness. He soon made the discovery that he could no longer move at all. This was no surprise to him, it seemed rather that being able to actually move around on those spindly little legs until then was unnatural. He also felt relatively comfortable. It is true that his entire body was aching, but the pain seemed to be slowly getting weaker and weaker and would finally disappear altogether. He could already hardly feel the decayed apple in his back or the inflamed area around it, which was entirely covered in white dust. He thought back of his family with emotion and love. If it was possible, he felt that he must go away even more strongly than his sister. He remained in this state of empty and peaceful rumination until he heard the clock tower strike three in the morning. He watched as it slowly began to get light everywhere outside the window too. Then, without his willing it, his head sank down completely, and his last breath flowed weakly from his nostrils.

When the cleaner came in early in the morning - they'd often asked her not to keep slamming the doors but with her strength and in her hurry she still did, so that everyone in the flat knew when she'd arrived and from then on it was impossible to sleep in peace - she made her usual brief look in on Gregor and at first found nothing special. She thought he was laying there so still on purpose, playing the martyr; she attributed all possible understanding to him. She happened to be holding the long broom in her hand, so she tried to tickle Gregor with it from the doorway. When she had no success with that she tried to make a nuisance of herself and poked at him a little, and only when she found she could shove him across the floor with no resistance at all did she start to pay attention. She soon realised what had really happened, opened her eyes wide, whistled to herself, but did not waste time to yank open the bedroom doors and shout loudly into the darkness of the bedrooms: "Come and 'ave a look at this, it's dead, just lying there, stone dead!"

Mr. and Mrs. Samsa sat upright there in their marriage bed and had to make an effort to get over the shock caused by the cleaner before they could grasp what she was saying. But then, each from his own side, they hurried out of bed. Mr. Samsa threw the blanket over his shoulders, Mrs. Samsa just came out in her nightdress; and that is how they went into Gregor's room. On the way they opened the door to the living room where Grete had been sleeping since the three gentlemen had moved in; she was fully dressed as if she had never been asleep, and the paleness of her face seemed to confirm this. "Dead?", asked Mrs. Samsa, looking at the charwoman enquiringly, even though she could have checked for herself and could have known it even without checking. "That's what I said", replied the cleaner, and to prove it she gave Gregor's body another shove with the broom, sending it sideways across the floor. Mrs. Samsa made a movement as if she wanted to hold back the broom, but did not complete it. "Now then", said Mr. Samsa, "let's give thanks to God for that". He crossed himself, and the three women followed his example. Grete, who had not taken her eyes from the corpse, said: "Just look how thin he was. He didn't eat anything for so long. The food came out again just the same as when it went in". Gregor's body was indeed completely dried up and flat, they had not seen it until then, but now he was not lifted up on his little legs, nor did he do anything to make them look away.

"Grete, come with us in here for a little while", said Mrs. Samsa with a pained smile, and Grete followed her parents into the bedroom but not without looking back at the body. The cleaner shut the door and opened the window wide. Although it was still early in the morning the fresh air had something of warmth mixed in with it. It was already the end of March, after all.

The three gentlemen stepped out of their room and looked round in amazement for their breakfasts; they had been forgotten about. "Where is our breakfast?", the middle gentleman asked the cleaner irritably. She just put her finger on her lips and made a quick and silent sign to the men that they might like to come into Gregor's room. They did so, and stood around Gregor's corpse with their hands in the pockets of their well-worn coats. It was now quite light in the room.

Then the door of the bedroom opened and Mr. Samsa appeared in his uniform with his wife on one arm and his daughter on the other. All of them had been crying a little; Grete now and then pressed her face against her father's arm.

"Leave my home. Now!", said Mr. Samsa, indicating the door and without letting the women from him. "What do you mean?", asked the middle of the three gentlemen somewhat disconcerted, and he smiled sweetly. The other two held their hands behind their backs and continually rubbed them together in gleeful anticipation of a loud quarrel which could only end in their favour. "I mean just what I said", answered Mr. Samsa, and, with his two companions, went in a straight line towards the man. At first, he stood there still, looking at the ground as if the contents of his head were rearranging themselves into new positions. "Alright, we'll go then", he said, and looked up at Mr. Samsa as if he had been suddenly overcome with humility and wanted permission again from Mr. Samsa for his decision. Mr. Samsa merely opened his eyes wide and briefly nodded to him several times. At that, and without delay, the man actually did take long strides into the front hallway; his two friends had stopped rubbing their hands some time before and had been listening to what was being said. Now they jumped off after their friend as if taken with a sudden fear that Mr. Samsa might go into the hallway in front of them and break the connection with their leader. Once there, all three took their hats from the stand, took their sticks from the holder, bowed without a word and left the premises. Mr. Samsa and the two women followed them out onto the landing; but they had had no reason to mistrust the men's intentions and as they leaned over the landing they saw how the three gentlemen made slow but steady progress down the many steps. As they turned the corner on each floor they disappeared and would reappear a few moments later; the further down they went, the more that the Samsa family lost interest in them; when a butcher's boy, proud of posture with his tray on his head, passed them on his way up and came nearer than they were, Mr. Samsa and the women came away from the landing and went, as if relieved, back into the flat.

They decided the best way to make use of that day was for relaxation and to go for a walk; not only had they earned a break from work but they were in serious need of it. So they sat at the table and wrote three letters of excusal, Mr. Samsa to his employers, Mrs. Samsa to her contractor and Grete to her principal. The cleaner came in while they were writing to tell them she was going, she'd finished her work for that morning. The three of them at first just nodded without looking up from what they were writing, and it was only when the cleaner still did not seem to want to leave that they looked up in irritation. "Well?", asked Mr. Samsa. The charwoman stood in the doorway with a smile on her face as if she had some tremendous good news to report, but would only do it if she was clearly asked to. The almost vertical little ostrich feather on her hat, which had been a source of irritation to Mr. Samsa all the time she had been working for them, swayed gently in all directions. "What is it you want then?", asked Mrs. Samsa, whom the cleaner had the most respect for. "Yes", she answered, and broke into a friendly laugh that made her unable to speak straight away, "well then, that thing in there, you needn't worry about how you're going to get rid of it. That's all been sorted out." Mrs. Samsa and Grete bent down over their letters as if intent on continuing with what they were writing; Mr. Samsa saw that the cleaner wanted to start describing everything in detail but, with outstretched hand, he made it quite clear that she was not to. So, as she was prevented from telling them all about it, she suddenly remembered what a hurry she was in and, clearly peeved, called out "Cheerio then, everyone", turned round sharply and left, slamming the door terribly as she went.

"Tonight she gets sacked", said Mr. Samsa, but he received no reply from either his wife or his daughter as the charwoman seemed to have destroyed the peace they had only just gained. They got up and went over to the window where they remained with their arms around each other.

Mr. Samsa twisted round in his chair to look at them and sat there watching for a while. Then he called out: "Come here, then. Let's forget about all that old stuff, shall we. Come and give me a bit of attention". The two women immediately did as he said, hurrying over to him where they kissed him and hugged him and then they quickly finished their letters.

After that, the three of them left the flat together, which was something they had not done for months, and took the tram out to the open country outside the town. They had the tram, filled with warm sunshine, all to themselves. Leant back comfortably on their seats, they discussed their prospects and found that on closer examination they were not at all bad - until then they had never asked each other about their work but all three had jobs which were very good and held particularly good promise for the future. The greatest improvement for the time being, of course, would be achieved quite easily by moving house; what they needed now was a flat that was smaller and cheaper than the current one which had been chosen by Gregor, one that was in a better location and, most of all, more practical. All the time, Grete was becoming livelier. With all the worry they had been having of late her cheeks had become pale, but, while they were talking, Mr. and Mrs. Samsa were struck, almost simultaneously, with the thought of how their daughter was blossoming into a well built and beautiful young lady. They became quieter. Just from each other's glance and almost without knowing it they agreed that it would soon be time to find a good man for her. And, as if in confirmation of their new dreams and good intentions, as soon as they reached their destination Grete was the first to get up and stretch out her young body.